VINCENT THE VERY VULGAR

Story by G Hake

Illustrations by J Sassi

For G and the real Ringo and Vincent

Special thanks to LB

Vincent was a Viking.
A vulgar Viking.
A very vulgar Viking.
He was a very vulgar Viking because
whenever he spoke to someone he was
very rude!

In the Very Far Away Land everybody was happy,
all of the time, until they met Vincent.
Vincent would **SHOUT** at them. He wasn't
very polite and he was always nasty. Even his
dog Ringo was extremely rude!

One day, King Royston, the Royal Righteous, heard about how rude Vincent had been. He told him the story of a place called "Nomanners' Land". It was a land where Vikings could live and be rude and nasty to whoever they met.

King Royston then gave Vincent a map to this land...

The very next day, Vincent and Ringo packed their boat to find "Nomanners' Land", with the map given to them by King Royston. They packed their favourite sandwiches, which were ragworm and banana skins!

"Let's go Ringo!" bellowed Vincent, as he cut the rope to set sail.

On the way, Vincent and Ringo sailed past many friendly birds. The birds would say "Good morning" to Vincent and Ringo, but all they did was be rude in return. **"Get out of our way!"** they would shout.

After **three days** of searching for Nomanners' Land, they began to get tired, sleepy and hungry. "I hope this map is right Ringo. I fear that we are lost!" said Vincent, as he ate the last of the ragworm and banana skin sandwiches.

As they drifted out to sea, they found a singing seagull. The seagull sang "Good morning" to Vincent and Ringo, but they were, as always, very rude back. **"Tell us where Nomanners' Land is!"** they shouted.
The seagull replied, "I'm sorry, but as you have been rude, I won't tell you", and he flew away.

Still they drifted and drifted.

The next day, they found a huge, happy whale.
The whale was very polite, "Good afternoon," he said to
Vincent and Ringo but, once again, they
were very rude to the whale.
 **"It's not a good afternoon, we've eaten all of our
sandwiches!"** shouted Vincent, **"now tell us
where Nomanners' Land is!"**
The whale replied and said, "I'm sorry, as
you're being very rude, I will not help you",
and away he swam.

Vincent and Ringo were
now very, very
tired; very, very hungry
and very, very
sleepy. They slept for the
whole of the next
day and were finally
awoken by a curly eel
saying "Good evening".
Vincent by now, was very
angry and shouted,
**"You've woken
me up! Now tell me how
to get to
Nomanners' Land!"**.
But the eel simply said,
"As you have been very
rude, I will not help
you," and he wriggled
away.

Vincent was now very angry and ripped up the map that King Royston had given him.

"Ringo, we've been searching for days and days; we're going to go back to the Very Far Away Land where everyone is happy, and I'm going to **shout** at King Royston. This map he gave us isn't any good!"

As Vincent began to turn the boat around,
they bumped into something very big.
Vincent, by now, was very angry and shouted,
"Ringo, what have we sailed into?"
Ringo looked out of the front of the boat,
and pointed to a sign that read "Nomanners'
Land".
"Ringo, we've found it! We've found
Nomanners' Land, we can be as rude as we
like to everyone we see!"
With that he jumped off the boat...

Ringo jumped off the boat too and both of
them ran across the sand, onto the land,
looking for someone to be rude to.
They ran and they ran, and they ran.
They ran some more, until they walked and
walked, and then...they stopped.

"Ringo, where is everyone? There's no one
here!" Vincent said, as he looked around.
Ringo looked around too, but couldn't see
anyone.

They were all alone, on Nomanners' Land,
with no one to be rude to.

Vincent began to feel sad, and Ringo was too.
They didn't like being on an island, on their
own, with no one else to talk to.
"What shall we do Ringo?" Vincent asked, as
he looked at the empty island. Ringo looked
at Vincent, and began to cry.
"Are you hungry Ringo?" Vincent enquired.
Ringo nodded and wagged his tail.
"Shall we go home Ringo?" said Vincent.
Ringo started to bark and wagged his tail
even more as he jumped back into the boat.

Vincent and Ringo left Nomanners' Land, but
they didn't know where to go, or how to get home.
As they set off, they saw the eel they spoke
to earlier that evening."Good evening eel,
could you tell us how to get back to the very far away
land please?"
"No" said the eel and he wriggled away.

The next day, the whale they had met previously went swimming past their boat.
"Good afternoon whale," Vincent said, "Could you help us get back to the Very Far Away Land, please? We are lost".
"No," replied the whale and swam away.
"Oh dear Ringo, we really are lost. What shall we do?".

The day after that, they saw the seagull
again, and asked for directions. "Good
morning seagull, would you be able to tell
us how to get home to the very far away land please?"
"No," replied the seagull, and he flew away.
"Oh dear Ringo, we are very very lost".
Ringo was sad as he missed home.

"I know Ringo, I miss home too", and they
both laid down to sleep, dreaming of home
and ragworm and banana skin sandwiches.

The next day, they were woken up by the
boat hitting a large rock. "What was that sound Ringo?"
Vincent said, as he rubbed his eyes.
Ringo pointed to a sign that said "The Very Far Away
Land".
"Ringo, we've made it home!" Vincent said as
he jumped off the boat and ran across the
sand.

Ringo jumped off the boat too and they ran and ran until...they ran into King Royston. "King Royston, we have returned from Nomanners' Land; it was nasty, it was horrible, it was lonely. Please can we live here, we promise never to be rude or cause upset to anyone ever again? Please, King Royston, please!" begged Vincent.

"I see", said King Royston, "so you found Nomanners' Land then?"

"Yes" said Vincent, "the map didn't help us, and everyone we spoke to wouldn't help us either. Also when we got there, it was lonely and empty. Please can we stay? Please!"

"Of course you can," said the King. "I hope you threw the map away?"

"I did," said Vincent.

"Good" replied the King, "as you won't be needing it any more. Welcome home!"

From that day forward, and from this day back, Vincent and Ringo we're polite and kind to **everyone** they met!

THE END

Lightning Source UK Ltd
Milton Keynes UK
UKOW07f0120120316

270079UK00001B/4/P